Poskitt's Puzz[...]

THE MYSTE[...]
THE PIRATE'S
TREASURE

by Kjartan Poskitt

Illustrated by David Higham

IDEALS CHILDREN'S BOOKS
Nashville, Tennessee

"Hello, I'm Benjamin. While searching for some treasure hidden on this island by my grandfather, I lost an old ring that he had given me. Can you help me find the ring?

"If I tell you all I can remember about my treasure hunt, we can retrace my steps. Then we'll be able to determine where and in what container each treasure was found. If we can figure that out, we should be able to find the ring."

(Hint: Pay attention to the visual clues as well as the words.)

First published in the United States by
Ideals Publishing Corporation
Nelson Place at Elm Hill Pike
Nashville, Tennessee 37214
in association with
Belitha Press Limited
31 Newington Green, London N16 9PU
Text and illustrations in this format © 1990 by
Belitha Press

Text copyright © 1990 by Kjartan Poskitt
Illustrations copyright © 1990 by David Higham
ISBN 0-8249-8417-X (softcover)
ISBN 0-8249-8416-1 (hardcover)
Printed in Hong Kong for Imago Publishing

"There were four treasures in four hiding places. I've marked them on the map on the following page.

"These silver plates were the first treasure I found.

Smuggler's Cottage

Trees of Wisdom

Green Pond

Silver Beach

"Each of the treasures was in a different type of container. The last treasure I found was in this Greek urn.

"I chipped the urn with my pick as I dug it up.

"The rubies were in this jewel box, but not all the
treasures were treated so carefully. For instance,
one of the treasures was in this old leather
bag.

"Another treasure was in this old chest buried on Silver Beach.

"These are the Trees of Wisdom. I found one of the treasures here.

"I found the second treasure in the Smuggler's Cottage.

"I used a long pole to fish a treasure out of the middle of Green Pond.

"I had to climb a ladder to get these pearls out of a bird's nest!

''These gold coins are called 'Pieces of Eight.'
When I think back, I'm *sure* I lost the ring when I
found the coins.

"That's all I can remember about my treasure hunt. From what you've seen and what I've told you, can you determine the order in which I found the treasures and where they were? Figuring out these hiding places will help you find the ring."

Hint: First determine what container the pearls were in, then the silver. Finally, figure out what container the gold was in and where the gold was located.

Now have you found the ring?

Stumped? Try working the puzzle again, paying close attention to the words and visual clues.

Give up? Send a self-addressed, stamped envelope to: Poskitt's Answers, Ideals Publishing Corporation, Nelson Place at Elm Hill Pike, P.O. Box 140300, Nashville, Tennessee 37214.